Wilmot Gibbes De Saussure

The Names of the Officers who Served in the South Carolina Regiments

on the continental establishment of the officers who served in the militia -

of what troops were upon the continental establishement

Wilmot Gibbes De Saussure

The Names of the Officers who Served in the South Carolina Regiments
on the continental establishment of the officers who served in the militia - of what
troops were upon the continental establishement

ISBN/EAN: 9783337409166

Printed in Europe, USA, Canada, Australia, Japan

Cover: Foto ©Andreas Hilbeck / pixelio.de

More available books at **www.hansebooks.com**

THE NAMES

AS FAR AS CAN BE ASCERTAINED OF THE

OFFICERS

WHO SERVED IN THE

SOUTH CAROLINA REGIMENTS

ON THE CONTINENTAL ESTABLISHMENT; OF THE OFFICERS
WHO SERVED IN THE MILITIA; OF WHAT TROOPS
WERE UPON THE CONTINENTAL ESTABLISH-
MENT; AND OF WHAT MILITIA OR-
GANIZATIONS SERVED;

TOGETHER WITH

SOME MISCELLANEOUS INFORMATION.

PREPARED BY

GENERAL WILMOT G. DeSAUSSURE.

PUBLISHED BY ORDER OF THE GENERAL ASSEMBLY, 1886.

Hon. John F. Ficken, Mayor of Charleston :—

DEAR SIR :—The paper mentioned in your note of 24th ulto., is :—"The names, as far as can be ascertained, of the Officers "who served in the South Carolina Regiments on the "Continental establishment : of the officers who served in the "militia : of what troops were upon the Continental estab- "lishment : and of what militia organizations served : together "with some miscellaneous information." It was prepared by my late father, Genl. Wilmot G. DeSaussure, President of "The State Society of the Cincinnati of South Carolina, pre- "sented by that Society, as a contribution * * * to the "history of the War of the Revolution in South Carolina," to the State through Governor Thompson, he transmitted it to the Legislature, and under concurrent resolution five hundred copies were printed in 1886, a limited number of these were distributed, the rest remained in the State Library. I believe copies were sent to the Congressional Library, Washington, D. C., but am uninformed whether copies were sent to the War Department.

With the paper was published the letter of presentation dated 28th Nov., 1884, Gov. Thompson's Message, No. 4, of 12th Dec., 1884 : and concurrent resolution, directing its pub- lication, adopted in 1884.

New Jersey had recently published a list of its soldiers of the Revolution. There was no collected record of the South Carolina troops in that war, neither continental nor militia, their names were scattered through the various histories of South Carolina and fragmentary State papers published ; the official records of the United States do not show what troops South Carolina furnished, showing, I believe, two regiments as its total contingent.

These and cogent reasons led to its preparation and presen- tation to the Cincinnati Society and by it to the State.

Its general interest historically, the limited edition, and dif- ficulty of procuring copies, seem to render re-publication opportune.

As desired, I enclose a copy of the pamphlet, and suggest the title page remain unaltered save by adding " Republished in Year Book 1893."

I am with much respect, your obedient servant,

HENRY A. DeSAUSSURE.

Charleston, S. C., June 14th, 1894.

LIST OF OFFICERS

OF THE SOUTH CAROLINA LINE, UPON THE CONTINENTAL ESTABLISHMENT, DURING THE WAR OF THE REVOLUTION, 1775-1783.

This list is made from the Journals of the Provincial Congress, so far as the same has been accessible; from the Journals of the Council of Safety, so far as the same have been accessible; from Moultrie Revolution, from Ramsay Revolution, from such orderly books of General William Moultrie and General Francis Marion as are accessible; from various books relating to the Revolution, from extracts from the revolutionary muster-rolls, &c., on file in the Department of State at Washington, and from whatever other sources of information on this subject could be gathered.

The list is doubtless imperfect, but so many names as are here gathered, are by this list preserved from oblivion.

In preparing this list, aid has been received from many friends, and acknowledgments are now made for such aid. Mrs. Lucy H. Pickens, Miss S. P. Brownfield, Major Asa Bud Gardner, U. S. A., Col. T. W. Woodward, Major Harry Hammond, Mr. Isaac Ball, Mr. W. Ederington, have all contributed to the names in this list. Major E. Willis, of Charleston, who has probably the largest and best collection in the State, of histories, pamphlets, &c., relating to the history of South Carolina, most kindly placed any and all of his collection at the disposal of the Society, and himself extracted and furnished a large number of names.

Adair, William	Lieutenant 6th Regiment	
Alexander Charles	" " "	
Alexander, Nathaniel	Surgeon's mate	
Anderson, David	Captain 5th Regiment	
Armstrong, John	" " "	Died 3d October, 1778.
Armstrong, Robert	Lieutenant 1st Regiment	
Armstrong, William	Major "	
Ashby, Anthony	Lieutenant 2d Regiment	Resigned Feb. 16, 1778.
Axson, Samuel J	Surgeon's mate	
Airs, ——	Surgeon	Died ——, 1777.
Bailey, ——	Lieutenant 3rd Regiment	Killed Savannah, 9th October, 1779.
Baker, Jesse	Captain " "	
Baker, Richard Bohun	" 2nd "	
Barnwell, John	" 1st "	Resigned, Dec. 11, 1775.
Beckman, Barnard	Colonel 4th Regiment Art'y	
Beckman, Samuel	Lieutenant — Regiment	
Belin, Allard	" 1st "	" 1777.

Name	Rank	Notes
Blake, John	Lieutenant 2d Regiment	Resigned April 25, 1778.
Blameyer, William	Captain 5th "	" Nov. 1778.
Bowie, John		[tober 1779.
Boyce, Alexander	" 6th "	Killed Savannah, 9th Oc-
Boykin, Francis	Lieutenant 3d Regiment	
Bradwell, Nathaniel	" 1st "	
Bremar, Francis	Dep. Must. Mast.	
Brown, Charles	Lieutenant 1st Regiment	
Brown, John	Captain 5th "	
Brown, Richard	" 3d "	
Brown, William	" 6th "	Resigned Dec. 1778
Brownfield, Robert	Surgeon's mate	
Brownson, Nathaniel	Dep. Sun. Med. Dep't	
Buchanan, John	Captain 3d Regiment	
Budd, John Shivers	Surgeon 4th Reg't Artillery	
Burke, Ædanus	Lieutenant 2d Regiment	Resigned 22d Feb., 1778.
Bush, John	" " "	Killed Savannah, 9th Oc-
Buchanan, ——	" " "	[tober, 1779.
Brown, Benjamin	" 6th "	
Baker, S	" " "	
Caddett, ——	Lieutenant — Regiment	
Caldwell, John	Captain 3d "	
Caldwell, William	" " "	
Cameron, Allan	Lieutenant " "	
Capers, William	" 2d "	
Carne, John	Ass't Dep't Apothecary	
*Caltell, Benjamin	Captain 1st Regiment	
*Caltell, William	" " "	
Charnock, William	" 2d "	Resigned Nov. 25, 1778.
Chesnut, John	Paymaster 3d Regiment	
Cleiland, John	Surgeon's mate 3d Reg't	
Cogdell, George	Captain 5th Reg't	
Coit, ——	" 6th "	Resigned Sept. 3, 1778.
Conyers, Clement	" 5th "	
Cooper, Leonard	" " "	
Crowther, Isaac	Lieutenant 3d Regiment	
Couterier, John	Capt. — Reg't Lt, Drag.	
Cole, ——	Ensign 2d "	
Daniel, John	Lieutenant — Regiment	
Dark, John Sandford	Paymaster 1st "	
Davis, Harman	Captain — "	
Davis, John	Lieutenant 3d "	
Davis, William Ransom	Captain 5th "	
DeBraham, ——	Major Engineers	
D'Ellient, Andrew	Brigade Major	[tober, 1779.
DeSaussure, Louis	Lieutenant 3d Regiment	Killed Savannah, 9th Oc-
DeTreville, John LaB	Captain 4th Reg't Art'y	
Deveaux, ——	"	
Dickenson, Benjamin	Lieutenant 1st Regiment	[1779.
Dixon, Henry	Brigade Inspector	Killed, Stono, June 20,
Doggatt, ——	Captain 6th Regiment	[tober, 1779.
Donaldson, James	Captain 3rd Regiment	Killed, Savannah, 9th Oc-
Donnom, William	" 4th Reg't Art'y	Resigned 6th October,
Downes, William	Adjutant 2nd Regiment	[1878.
D'Oyley, Daniel	Captain 1st Regiment	
Drayton, Charles	" 4th Reg't Ar'y	
Drayton, Glen	Lieutenant 2nd Regiment	Resigned August, 1779.
Drayton, Stephen	Dep. Quartermaster Gen'l	
Dubose, Isaac	Lieutenant 2nd Regiment	[tober, 1779.
Dubois, David	Captain — Reg't Drag.	Killed, Savannah, 9th Oc-
Duff, James	" 6th Regiment	
Dunbar, Thomas	Lieutenant 2d Regiment	
Dunham, ——	Captain 4th Reg't Art'y	
Dutarque, Louis	Lieutenant 3d Regiment	Resigned Jan. 30, 1776.
Doggatt, Joel	" 6th "	
Earle, Samuel	Captain 5th Regiment	
Edmunds, David	Lieutenant — Regiment	
Elliott, Barnard	Lieut. Col. 4th "	Died 5th October, 1778.
Elliott, Joseph	Lieutenant 1st "	Died.
Elliot, Thomas	" 2d "	
Esum, John	Adjutant 3d "	
Evance, Thomas	Paymaster 2d "	Died 18th Dec., 1777.
Evans, George	Lieutenant " "	
Eveleigh, George	" " "	Died ——, 1777.
Eveleigh, Michael	Captain — "	Probably a mistake for
Eveleigh, Nicolas	Dep. Adjutant General	[Nicholas Eveleigh

* So in printed pamphlet, but believed to be misprint for Caltell.

Edmunds, David	Lieutenant — Regiment	Died ——, 1778.
Far, John	Lieutenant 2d Regiment	
Farrar, Field	Captain 3d "	
Farrar, Thomas	Lieutenant — "	
Fayssoux, Peter	Paymaster and Surgeon	
Ferguson, ——	Major 3d Regiment	
Field, James	Lieut. 4th Reg't Art'y	
Fildboath, ——	" " " "	
Fisby, ——	Lieut. 2d Bat. Lt. Inf'y	
Fishburne, William	Lieutenant 1st Regiment	
Fitzpatrick, William	" 3d "	Resigned Aug. 24. 1778.
Flagg, Henry C.	Surgeon — "	
Foissin, Peter	Lieutenant 2d Regiment	[15th March, 1781.
Forbes, John	Captain — "	Killed, Guilford C. H.,
Ford, Tobias	Lieutenant — Regiment	
Fraser, Alexander	" 1st "	
Frierson, John	" 2d "	
Fuller, Richard	" 1st "	Died.
Gadsden, Christopher	Brigadier General	Resigned ——, 1777.
Gadsden, Thomas	Captain 1st Regiment	
Galvan, William	Lieutenant 2d Regiment	Resigned 5th July, 1778.
Garden, Alexander	Cornet Lee's Legion	[tober, 1779.
Gaston, Robert	Lieutenant 3d Regiment	Killed, Savannah, 9th Oc-
Gervais, John Lewis	Dep. Paym'r Gen. S. Dep.	
Giles, Thomas	Capt. — Reg't Lt. Drag.	
Glover, Wilson	Lieutenant 1st Regiment	
Goodwyn, John	Captain " "	
Goodwyn, John	" 4th Reg't Art'y	
Goodwyn Richard	Capt. — Reg't Lt. Drag.	
Goodwyn, Robert	Captain 3d Regiment	Resigned May 30, 1778.
Goodwyn, Uriah	" 2d "	
Goodwyn, William	Lieutenant 3d Regiment	Resigned May 30, 1778.
Gray, George	" 1st "	Lost on schr Randolph.
Gray, Henry	" 2d "	Resigned Dec. 15, 1777.
Gray, James	" " "	Killed, Savannah, 9th
Gray, Peter	Captain 2d "	[October, 1779.
Grayson, John	Lieut. 4th Reg't Art'y	
Grimke, John F	Lieut. Col Dep. Adj. Gen.	
Guerry, Samuel	Lieutenant 2d Regiment	Died 12th July, 1779.
Guerry, Stephen	Captain 5th "	Resigned August, 1779.
Gould, ——	Surgeon 1st Regiment	
Gordon, ——	Lieutenant 5th Regiment	
Hall, John	Quartermaster 2d Reg't	
Hall, Thomas	Captain " "	
Hambleton, ——	Lieutenant — "	
Hamilton, John	" 1st "	
Hampton, John	Capt. — Reg't Lt. Drag.	
Hampton, Richard	Lt. Col. — Reg't Lt. Drag.	
Hampton, Wade	" " " " "	
Hardaway, Joel	Lieutenant 1st Regiment	
Harleston, Isaac	Major 6th "	
Harthorn, Joseph	Captain 6th "	Resigned Aug. 9, 1778.
Hart, John	" 2d "	
Hart, Oliver	Surgeon	
Hazzard, William	Lieutenant 1st Regiment	
Healtey, Charles	" 3d "	Resigned Jan. 30, 1776.
Heard, John	Lt. Fireworker 4th Reg't	
Henderson, William	Lieut. Col. 6th Regiment	
Hennenton, John	Lieutenant " "	
Hext, William	Captain 1st "	
Hodges, Benjamin	Lieutenant 3d "	
Hogan, ——	Captain 5th "	
Hopkins, David	" 1st "	
Horry, Daniel	" " "	
Horry, Peter	Lieut. Col. 2d "	
Hourston, James	Surgeon	[May, 1779.
Huger, Benjamin	Major 5th Regiment	Killed, Charlestown, 11th
Huger, Francis	Captain 1st Regiment	
Huger, Isaac	Brigadier General	
Hughes, Henry	Lieutenant 1st Regiment	[October, 1779.
Hume, Alexander	" 2d "	Killed, Savannah, 9th
Hyrne, Edmund	Lieut. Col Dep. Adj. Gen.	
Heyward, William	Lieutenant 1st Regiment	Resigned 22d Oct., 1777.

Hampton, Henry	Captain 6th Regiment	
Imhoff, John L. S.	Lieutenant 3d Regiment	
Joor, Joseph	Lieutenant 2d Regiment.	Lost on schr. Randolph
Jackson, Bazil	" — "	
Jackson, William	Captain 1st "	
Jenkins, Joseph	Lieutenant 1st "	
Jewey, Thomas	Capt. Dep. Must. Mast.	Resigned Nov. 1778.
Johnson, Robert	Hospital Physician	
Jones, John	Lieutenant 3d Regiment	
Jones Richard	" " "	
Jervey, ——	Captain 5th "	
Jones, ——	Lieutenant 5th "	
*Kaltiesen, Michel	Capt. Wagonmaster Gen'l	
Knap, John	Lieutenant 1st Regiment	
Keith, Alexander	Capt. 3d "	
Kennedy, James	Lieutenant 1st "	
Kershaw, Ely	Captain 3d "	Resigned October, 1777.
Kirkland, Moses		
Kobb, Josiah	Lieutenant 2d "	
Lacy, James	Lieutenant 6th Regiment	Died December 20, 1778.
Ladson, James	" 2d "	
Langford, Daniel		
Laurens, John	Lieut. Col. of D. C	Killed, Combahee, Aug.
Legare, James	Lieutenant 2d Regiment	[27, 1781].
Lesesne, Thomas	Captain " "	Resigned 6th Aug. 1779.
Levacher, St. Marie	" 1st "	
Liddell, George	Lieutenant 3d "	
Lining, Charles	Captain 1st "	
Leston, Thomas	Lieutenant — Regiment	
Lisle, John	" 3d "	Resigned August, 1779.
Lloyd, Benjamin	" " "	
Lloyd Edward	" " "	
Lochman, John	Surgeon	
Lyell, Robert	Captain 3d Regiment	
Lynch, Thomas, Jr	" 1st "	
La Marzell, ——	Lieutenant 4th Regiment	Resigned ——, 1777.
Love, William	" 3d "	
Maham, Hezekiah	Capt. 5th Reg't Lt. Col. Regiment Light Drag.	
Marion, Francis	Lieut. Col. 2d Regiment	
Marion, Gabriel, Jr	Lieutenant " "	Killed ——, 1781.
Martin, James	Surgeon	
Martin, John	Captain 2d Regiment	
Mason, Luke	Lieutenant 3d Regiment	
Mason, Richard	Captain 2d "	
Mason, William	" 1st "	
Massey, William	Adjutant 1st "	
Mayson, James	Lieut. Col. 3d "	
Mazyck, Daniel	Captain 2d "	
Mazyck, Stephen	Lieutenant 2d "	
McDonald, Adam	Captain 1st "	Died ——, 1778.
McDonald, James	" " "	
McGinnis, Charles	Lieutenant — Regiment	
McGuire, Merry	" 2d "	
McIntosh, Alexander	Major " "	
McQueen, Alexander	Lieutenant 1st "	
Middleton, Hugh	" 3d "	
Middleton, John	Cornet Lee's Legion	
Milling, Hugh	Capt. Lieut. 6th Regiment	
Mitchell, Ephraim	Major — Regiment	
Mitchell, James	Captain 4th Reg't Art'y	
Mitchell, William	Lt. Fireworker 4th Reg't	
Monaghan, David	Lieutenant 3d Regiment	Resigned 24th, ——, 1775.
Moore, Francis	Major	
Moore, Henry	Lieut. 4th Reg't Art'y	[October, 1779.
Motte, Charles	Captain 2d Regiment	Killed, Savannah, 9th
Motte, Isaac	Lieut. Col. 2d Regiment	Resigned Sept. 23, 1778.
Monalt, William	Captain 1st "	Resigned ——, 1777.
Moultrie, Thomas	" 2d "	Killed, Charlestown,
Moultrie, William	Major General	[May, 1780.
Moultrie, William	Lieutenant 2d Regiment	

*So in printed pamphlet, but should be " Michael Kalteissen."

Mowatt, John	Lieutenant 1st	"
Marshall, ——	Captain 2d	"
Monterip, Richard	Lieutenant 5th	"
McNeill, Daniel	Surg. mate 2d	"
Marshall, Thomas	Captain 3d Regiment	
McKinney, James	Lieutenant 5th	"
Nelson, John	Major	
Neufville, William	Regimental Surgeon	
Newson, Benjamin	Lieutenant 2d Regiment	[May, 1780.
Neyle, Philip	" 1st "	Killed, Charlestown,
Nixon, George	Adjutant 4th Reg't Art'y	
Ogier, George	Lieutenant 2d Regiment	
Oliphant, David	Medical Director	
Oliphant, William	Lieutenant 2d Regiment	Resigned Oct. 20, 1777.
Ousby, Thomas	" — "	
Paggett, ——	Captain — Regiment	
Parham, ——	Lieutenant 1st Regiment	
Parsons, ——	" 5th "	
Partridge, William	" 1st "	
Peronneau, Henry	" 2d "	Resigned July 15, 1778.
Peronneau, James	" 1st "	
Petrie, Alexander	Captain 5th "	Resigned 8th Oct. 1778.
Petrie, George (worth	Lieutenant 2d "	
Pinckney, Chas. Cotes-	Colonel 1st "	
Pinckney, Thomas	Major "	
Platen, Frederick Von	Lieut. 4th Reg't Ar'ty	
Pledger, Joseph	Lieutenant 3d Regiment	Resigned Jan. 30, 1776.
Polk, Ezekiel	Captain " "	
Pollard, Richard	" " "	
Postell, Benjamin	Lieutenant 1st "	
Potts, Thomas	Captain 5th "	
Poyas, John E	Hospital mate	
Prescott, Joseph	Surgeon	
Prince, Francis	Captain 5th Regiment	
Provaux, Adrian	" 2d "	
Purcell, Henry, Rev	Brigade Chaplain	
Purvis, John	Captain 3d Regiment	
Peronneau, John	Lieutenant 2d Regiment	Resigned Dec. 12, 1777,
Ramsay, Henry	Lieutenant —— Regiment	
Ramsay, Joseph H	Surgeon	
Rasche, John Henry	Surgeon's mate 2d Reg't	
Rayford, ——	Captain —— Regiment	
Read, William	Physician and Surgeon	
Redmond, ——	Lieutenant 6th Regiment	
Richardson, Edward	Captain 3d "	Resigned Jan 30, 1776,
Richardson, Richard, Jr	" 6th "	[1779.
Richardson, William	" 5th "	Killed, Stono, 20th June,
Roberts, Owen	Colonel 4th Reg't Artillery	
Roberts, Richard Brooks	Captain " "	
Roberson, James	Lieutenant 3d Regiment	
Rodgers, Alexander	Surgeon 3d "	
Rogers, Christopher, Jr	Lieutenant 2d "	
Rose, Hugh	Surgeon " "	
Rothmaler, Erasmus	Lieutenant — "	
Roux, Albert	Captain 2d "	
Russell, Thos. Com'ndr	Lieutenant 1st "	
Raphel, ——	Lieut 4th Reg't Art'y	Died October, 1777.
Rolando, ——	" 5th "	Resigned ——, 1777.
Rutledge, Andrew	Dep. Wagonmaster Gen'l	
Sanders, Roger Parker	Captain 1st Regiment	Resigned 8th Oct. 1778.
Schreiber, Jacob	" Engineers	
Scott, William	Lieut Col — Regiment	
Screven, Benjamin	Capt — Reg't Lt Drag	
Senf, Christian	Captain Engineers	
Shubrick, Jacob	Lieutenant 2d Regiment	Died 27th April, 1778.
Shubrick, Richard		Died 8th Nov, 1777,
Shubrick, Thomas	Captain " "	
Simons, James	Cornet Lee's Legion	
Singleton, Richard	Lieutenant 1st Regiment	

Name	Rank	Notes
Skirving, Charles	Lieutenant 1st Regiment	
Smith, Aaron	" 2d "	
Smith, Daniel	Dep Med Surveyor	
Smith, John Caraway	Captain 2d Regiment	
Smith, Press	Lieutenant 1st Regiment	
Smith, Robert, Rt Rev	Hospital Chaplain	
Smith, Samuel	Lieutenant 1st Regiment	Resigned August, 1779.
Springer, Sylvester	Surgeon's mate, 2d Regiment	
Stevens, Wm S	Junior Surgeon	
Sumter, Thomas	Lieut Col 6th Regiment	Resigned Sept. 23, 1778,
Sunu, Frederick	Reg't Surgeon, —— Reg't	
Shackelford, ——	Captain 5th "	Resigned 7th Dec, 1777.
Spencer, ——	" " "	
Simons, ——	Lieutenant —— Regiment	Lost on schr Randolph
Simpson, Robert	Adjutant 5th Regiment	Resigned Nov, 1778.
Taggart, William	Lieutenant 3d Regiment	
Tate, Wm	Capt Lieut 5th "	Resigned 22d Dec. 1777.
Taylor, Samuel	Major 6th "	
Theus, Jeremiah	Surgeon 2d "	
Thens, Simeon	Captain 1st "	
Thompson, William	Colonel 3d "	
Thompson, ——	Lieutenant 3d "	
Towles, Oliver	Captain " "	
Townsend, Paul	Paymaster 4th Reg't Artil'ry	
Tucker, Thomas Tudor	Physician and Surgeon	
Turner, George	Captain 1st Regiment	
Tutt, Benjamin	" 5th "	
Tutt, Richard	" " "	
Taylor, Thomas	" 3d "	Resigned October, 1777.
Valentine, Wm	Lieutenant 1st Regiment	
Vanderhorst, James	" —— "	
Vanderhorst, John	Major 2d "	
Vaughan, ——	Surgeon	[October, 1779.
Vileland, Cornelius Van	Lieutenant 2d "	Killed, Savannah, 9th.
Vickars, Samuel	Hospital Physician	
Wage, George	Captain 6th Regiment	
Wallace, John	Surgeon	
Walter, John Allen	Lieutenant 2d Regiment	
Ward, John Peter	" 1st "	
Ward, Wm	" , "	
Warley, Felix	Captain 1st "	
Warley, George	" 2d "	
Warley, Joseph	" " "	
Warley, Paul	Lieutenant " "	Resigned —— 1777.
Warren, Samuel	Captain 5th "	
Watson, Samuel	Lieutenant 3d "	
West, Cato	" " "	Resigned Sept. 14, 1778.
White, Sims	Captain 4th Regt Art'ly	Resigned ——, 1777.
Wickley, John	" — Regiment	[October, 1779.
Wickom, John	Ensign 2d "	Killed, Savannah, 9th
Williamson, John	Captain 1st "	
Wilson, ——	Capt Lt 4th Reg't Art'ly	
Wilson, ——	Lieutenant " "	[October, 1779.
Winn, Richard	Lieutenant 3d Regiment	Killed, Savannah, 9th
Wise, Samuel	Major " "	
Withers, William R	Ensign — " "	
Woodward, Thomas	Captain 3d "	Resigned Jan, 30, 1779,
Walsh, Edward	" 5th "	Resigned May 30, 1778.

TROOPS OF SOUTH CAROLINA, UPON THE CONTI-
NENTAL ESTABLISHMENT DURING THE WAR
OF THE REVOLUTION, 1775–1782.

Resolution of the Continental Congress, 15th June, 1775.

" *Resolved,* That a General be appointed to command all
the Continental forces raised, or to be raised, for the defence
of American liberty."

Order of General George Washington, 4th July, 1775.

" The Continental Congress having now taken all the
troops of the several Colonies which have been raised, or
which may be hereafter raised, for the support and defence
of the liberties of America, into their pay and service, they
are now the troops of the United Provinces of North America ; and it is hoped that all distinction of Colonies will be
laid aside, so that one and the same spirit may animate the
whole, and the only contest be, who shall render, on this
great and trying occasion, the most essential service to
the great and common cause in which we are all engaged."
" By his Commission, he was invested with the command
over all forces raised, or to be raised, by the United Colonies, and with full power and authority to act as he should
think good for the good and welfare of the service."
Bancroft's Hist. U. S., Vol. VII., p. 402, Chap.
XXXVII.

1775. " Besides the Regiments included in these two
armies, Congress had already taken into Colonial pay the
three regiments of South Carolina, presently increased to
five." &c.
Hildreth's Hist. U. S., Vol. III., p. 109, Chap. XXXII.

1776. "All the hitherto scattered Continental forces
were to be embraced in one grand whole, to consist of 88

Battalions of 750 men each. Battalions being substituted for regiments, to get rid of the rank of Colonel, which had occasioned difficulty about exchanges. Hazen's Canadian Regiment was also to be kept up, to be recruited in any of the States, and hence known as 'Congress's own.' Massachusetts and Virginia were each to furnish 15 Battalions: Pennsylvania, 12: North Carolina, 9; Connecticut, 8: South Carolina, 6; New York and New Jersey, 4 each: New Hampshire and Maryland, 3 each; Rhode Island, 2; Delaware and Georgia, each, 1."

Hildreth's Hist. U.S., Vol. III., p. 164, Chap. XXXV.

General Assembly of South Carolina, 20th September, 1776.

" *Resolved,* That this House do acquiesce in the Resolutions of the Continental Congress of the 18th of June and the 24th of July last, relative to the putting of two Regiments of Infantry, the Regiment of Rangers, the Regiment of Artillery, and two Regiments of Riflemen, in the service of this State, upon the Continental Establishment."

Moultrie's Revolution, Vol. I., p. 187.

Provincial Congress of South Carolina, 5th June, 1775.

On our first meeting, they determined upon a defensive war; and on the fourth day it was resolved to raise two Regiments of 500 men each. * * * The day after the officers of the first and second Regiments of foot were ballotted for, it was resolved to raise a Regiment of Cavalry Rangers of 500 men.

Field Officers of the First Regiment.

Christopher Gadsden, Colonel.

Isaac Huger, Lieut. Colonel.   Owen Roberts, Major.

Captains— Charles C. Pinckney,   Benjamin Cattell,
    William Cattell,   Edmund Hyrne,
    Thomas Lynch,   William Scott,
    John Barnwell,   Roger Parker Saunders
    Adam McDonald,   Thomas Pinckney.

First Lieutenants—
John Monat,   Alexander McQueen,
Thomas Elliott,   Benjamin Dickenson,
Glen Drayton,   Joseph Joor,
Richard Singleton,   Richard Armstrong,
John Vanderhorst,   James Ladson.

Field Officers of the Second Regiment.

William Moultrie, Colonel.
Isaac Motte, Lieut. Colonel.   Alexander McIntosh, Major.
Captains—Barnard Elliott,   James McDonald,
    Francis Marion,   Peter Horry,
    Daniel Horry,   Nicholas Eveleigh,
    Francis Huger,   Isaac Harleston,
    William Mason,   Charles Motte.
First Lieutenants—
    Richard Shubrick,   Richard Fuller,
    John Allen Walter,   William Chamock.
    William Oliphant,   Anthony Ashby,
    Thomas Moultrie,   John Blake,
    Thomas Lesesne,   James Peronneau.

Field Officers of the Regiment of Rangers (3rd Regiment.)

William Thompson, Lieutenant-Colonel.
James Mayson, Major.
Captains—Samuel Wise,   Thomas Woodward,
    Ely Kershaw,   John Caldwell,
    Edward Richardson,   Moses Kirkland,
    Ezekial Polk,   John Purvis,
    Robert Goodwyn.
                Moultrie Revolution, Vol. I., p. 64.
        Gibbes Documentary History, 1764-76, p. 104.

Provincial Congress of South Carolina, 13th November, 1775.

"*Resolved*, That as there is a great of want of men to man-
age and fire the artillery in Fort Johnson and the other

fortifications now erected, and such batteries as it may hereafter be thought necessary to erect, a Regiment of Artillery be forthwith raised and embodied, to serve either in garrison or otherwise, by land or water, as the service of the Colony may require, to consist of three companies of 100 men each, including non-commissioned officers and gunners."

Field Officers of the Regiment of Artillery (4th Regiment.)

Owen Roberts, Lieutenant Colonel, Commandant.
Barnard Elliott, Major.
Captains—Barnard Beckman,   Sims White.
Charles Drayton,
Paymaster—Paul Townshend.   Surgeon—John Budd.
Moultrie Revolution, Vol. I, p. 93.
Journal of Provincial Congress, pp. 86, 84.

1776. March. Congress resolved to raise two Regiments of Riflemen.

Field Officers of First Regiment of Riflemen (5th Regiment.)

Isaac Huger, Colonel.
Alexander McIntosh, Lieutenant Colonel.
Benjamin Huger, Major.
Captains—Hezekiah Maham,   John Brown,
Benjamin Tutt,   Francis Prince,
George Cogdell,   David Anderson,
William Richardson,   Thomas Potts.

Field Officers of the Second Regiment of Riflemen (6th Regiment.)

Thomas Sumter, Lieutenant Colonel.
William Henderson, Major.
Captains—James Duff,   George Wage,
Richard Richardson, Jr.,   William Brown.
Samuel Taylor,

South Carolina had, also, the following enlisted troops in the field from time to time, but whether such troops were upon the Continental Establishment it is impracticable, with the present information, to say.

These troops certainly served under the Continental general officers, and, from such returns as are accessible, seem to have been regarded by such officers as parts of the regular troops. In General Moultrie's enumeration of Continental officers taken prisoners at the capitulation of Charleston, 12th May, 1780, he certainly enumerates as Continental officers one captain and one lieutenant, "Horry's Horse"

General Assembly of South Carolina.

No. 1119. An Ordinance for raising and supporting a Regiment of Light Dragoons for the public service.

Passed February 19, 1779. Too much obliterated to be copied.

Statutes at Large of So. Ca., Vol. IV, p. 470.

1779. Every effort was made to strengthen the Continental Army. Additional bounties and greater emoluments were promised as inducements to encourage the recruiting service. The extent and variety of military operations in the open country pointed out the advantages of cavalry. A Regiment of Dragoons was therefore ordered to be raised, in which the following appointments took place:

Daniel Horry, Colonel.
Captains—John Conturier,
John Hampton,
Benjamin Screven,

Hezekiah Maham, Major.
Richard Gough,
Thomas Giles,
Isaac Dubose.

Ramsay's Revolution, Vol. II, p. 3.

After Major General Nathaniel Greene assumed command in South Carolina, the General Assembly being unable to meet and provide its quota for the Continental army, because the State was overrun by British forces, it became in the judgment of General Greene, necessary to enlist some regular troops for and in the name of the State, which enlisted regular troops should take the places of those troops on the Continental Establishment, which had been annihilated by the capitulation of Charleston, 12th May, 1780.

It is with the information now possessed, impracticable to say how far General Greene was authorized to act, or whether what he did, had the effect of placing such enlisted troops upon the Continental Establishment. He appears to have regarded such troops as in the Continental service. In February, 1782, he wrote to Col. Peter Horry, who had enlisted one of the Regiments of Light Horse under such authority : " You will please make me an exact return of your non-commissioned officers and men, the term of service they are engaged for, and the conditions of bounty and pay ; also the number of your horses, clothing and accoutrements of every kind. I am making out a general report to Gen. Washington and the Minister of War of the state and condition of the forces of the Southern Department ; the returns are wanted immediately."

Gen. Marion writing on 1st August, 1781, to Col. Peter Horry, says :—" As you are getting clothing for your men on Continental expense."

Gen. Greene, writing to Gen. Marion of Col. Maham's command, on 16th January, 1782, says :—" My intention with respect to that corps was, that it should stand upon the same footing as Lieut. Col. Lee's Legion, which is called an independent corps."

The troops raised under Gen. Greene's authority appear to have been as follows :—

" In March, 1781, Gen. Sumter, with the approbation of Gen. Greene, raised three small regiments of regular State troops."

About the same time, as appears by the correspondence in Gibbes's Documentary History, 1781-1782, the following regiments of Light Horse were enlisted under Gen. Greene's authority :—

One under the command of Col. Peter Horry.
One   "   "   Col. Hezekiah Maham.
One   "   "   Col. Henry Hampton.
One   "   "   Col. Wade Hampton.
One   "   "   Col. —— Middleton.

If these enlisted troops are to be considered as parts of the South Carolina Troops upon the Continental Establishment, then during the Revolutionary War, South Carolina furnished fifteen Regiments to the Continental Army.

Resolutions of Continental Congress, 3rd and 21st October, 1780 : * * * "That the several States furnish the following quotas, viz. : * * * South Carolina, two Regiments of Infantry."

Revolutionary Orders of Washington, p. 129.

" By a resolve of Congress, passed when Gen. Gates took command of the Southern Department, power was vested in him to draw from the States within his Department the contingent of men and money which they were bound to contribute to the common cause. * * * The same powers were now transferred to Greene."

Johnson's Life of Greene, Vol. I, p. 329.

" A little time after we were in possession of Fort Johnson (15th September, 1775) it was thought necessary to have a flag for the purpose of signals (as there was no national or State flag at that time,) I was desired by the Council of Safety to have one made; upon which, as the State troops were clothed in blue, and the fort was garrisoned by the First and Second Regiments, who wore a silver crescent on the front of their caps, I had a large blue flag made with a crescent on the dexter corner, to be in uniform with the troops. This was the first American flag which was displayed in South Carolina. On its being first hoisted, it gave some uneasiness to our timid friends, who were looking forward to a reconciliation ; they said it had the appear-

2

ance of a declaration of war: and Capt. Thornborough, in the Tamar sloop of war, lying in Rebellion Road, would look upon it as an insult and a flag of defiance, and he would certainly attack the fort; but he knew his own force, and knew the weight of our metal, he therefore kept his station and contented himself with spying on us."

Moultrie's Revolution, Vol. I, p. 80.

Extract from Capt. F. Marion's Orderly Book, 1775.

" Regimental Orders by Col. Moultrie :

" Every officer to provide himself with a blue coatee, faced and cuffed with scarlet cloth, and lined with scarlet ; white buttons ; and white waistcoat and breeches, (a pattern may be seen at Mr. Trezevant's ;) also, a cap and black feather."

Gibbes's Documentary History, 1764–1776, p. 104.

Resolutions of Congress, and Orders from General Washington.

" HEAD QUARTERS, SHULT'S HILL, June 18th, 1780.

" As it is, at all times, of great importance, both for the sake of appearance and for regularity of service, that the different military ranks should be distinguished from each other, and more especially at the present, the Commander in Chief has thought proper to establish the following distinctions, and strongly recommends to all the officers to endeavor to conform with them as speedily as possible :

" The Major Generals to wear a blue coat with buff facings and linings, yellow buttons, white or buff underclothes, two epaulets with two stars upon each, and a black and white feather in the hat.

" The Brigadier Generals the same uniforms as the Major Generals, with the difference of one star instead of two, and a white feather.

" The Colonels, Lieutenant Colonels, and Majors, the uniforms of their Regiments, and two epaulets : Captains, the uniform of their Regiments, and an epaulet on their right shoulder; the Subalterns, the uniforms of their Regiments, and an epaulet on the left shoulder.

"The Aide-de-Camps, the uniform of their rank and corps, or, if they belong to no corps, the uniform of their general officers; those of the Major Generals and Brigadier Generals to wear a green feather in their hats; those of the Commander in Chief, white and green.

"The Inspectors, as well Sub as Brigade, the uniform of their rank and corps, with a blue feather in the hat.

"The corps of Engineers, and that of Sappers and Miners, a blue coat with buff facings, buff underclothes, and the epaulets of their rank: such of the Staff as have military rank, to wear the uniform of the rank and the corps to which they belong in the line; such as have no military rank, to wear a plain blue coat, with cockade and sword.

"All officers, as well warranted as commissioned, to wear side arms, either swords or genteel bayonets.

"By order of his Excellency,
GENERAL WASHINGTON.
"SCAMMEL, Adjutant General."
Moultrie Revolution. Vol. II., p. 361.

On 14th June, (1777) Congress " *Resolved*, That the flag of the thirteen United States be thirteen stripes, alternate red and white; that the union be thirteen stars, white in a blue field, representing a new constellation." Since that time, we have added a star for every new State.

Lossing's Field Book of the Revolution, Vol. 1, p. 192, note 1.

The New England Flag, under which the battle of Bunker Hill was fought, was blue, and one corner was quartered by the Red Cross of St. George, in one section of which was the Pine Tree.

On the 1st January, 1776, the new Continental Army was organized, and on that day the Union Flag of thirteen stripes was unfurled, for the first time, in the American camp at Cambridge. This Flag bore the device of the English Union which distinguishes the royal standard of

Great Britain. It is composed of the Cross of St. George to denote England, and the St. Andrew's Cross. in the form of an X to denote Scotland. * * * It was a year and a half later (and a year after the colonies were declared independent States) that, by official orders. "thirteen white stars upon a blue field" was a device substituted for the British Union, and then "the stars and stripes became our national banner."
Lossing's Field Book of the Revolution, Vol. 1, p. 511, note 1, p. 570, p. 577. note 1*.

Extract from Lieut. Col. Marion's Order Book, 12th June, 1778.

Ordered that the officers do immediately provide themselves with leather caps agreeable to a pattern fixed on and left with Mr. Colligan, Saddler, King Street, Charleston, and that they wear no other kind of caps.

Journal of Provincial Congress, 21st November, 1775.

Resolved, That the commissioned officers of the Colony regular troops take precedence of officers of equal degree in the Militia, without regard to prior dates of commissions in the latter: *Provided, nevertheless,* That a Second Lieutenant in the Regulars shall be subordinate to a First Lieutenant in the Militia, and so on in gradation in the Regulars and Militia respectively; that the precedency in the Regular forces be according to the number and denomination of the regiments of infantry and rangers, and the regiment of artillery, according to the custom of the British army; that all corps of Regulars take precedence of all corps of Militia, and that the regiments of Militia shall take precedence in the following manner:

1. Berkeley County.
2. Charles Town.
3. Granville County,

4. Colleton County.

5. Craven County, the lower part.

6. Orangeburg.

7. Craven County, the upper part.

8. Camden.

9. Ninety-Six, north of the Fish Dam Ford and between Enoree, Broad and Saludy Rivers.

10. The New Acquisition, south of the Fish Dam Ford and between Broad and Saludy Rivers, north of Enoree and between Broad and Saludy Rivers.

The following are the names of various different Military militia organizations which existed at and during the Revolutionary War. These names are taken from the various authorities cited, as the authorities from whom the names of the Militia officers hereinafter given are taken, to wit:

Charles Town Battalion of Artillery. Charles Town. 2 companies.

Charles Town Volunteers.   Charles Town.
Charles Town Light Infantry.   "   "
Charles Town Fusileers, German.   "   "
True Blue Company.   "   "
Grenadier Company.   "   "
Cannon's Company of Volunteers. "   "
Charles Town Rangers.   "   "
Beaufort Light Infantry.   Beaufort.
Beaufort Artillery.   "
Beaufort Company of Volunteers. Beaufort.
St. Helena Volunteers.
Euhaw Volunteers.
Huspa Volunteers.
Foot Rangers or Rovers, Raccoon Company.
James Island Company.
Salt Catcher Company.
Horry's Light Dragoons, — Regiment. State troops enlisted.

Maham's Light Dragoons,—Regiment. State troops, enlisted.
Wade Hampton's Light Dragoons—Reg't   "   "   ❦
Richard Hampton's "   "   "   "   "   ";
Boykin's Company of Catawba Indians.
Round O Volunteers.
Pon Pon Company.
Dozier's Company of Volunteers.
Indian Field Company.
Postell's Company's of Volunteers.
Edisto Island Volunteers.
John's Island Company.
Kingstree Company.
Stono Company.
Militia Rangers Volunteers.
Wando Company, Christ Church.
Port's Company of Volunteers.
St. George's Company.
Georgetown Artillery, Georgetown.
Light Horse, or Pocotaligo Hunters.
Oakely Creek Company.
St. Peter's Company.
Black Swamp Company.
Pipe Creek Company.
Boggy Gut Company.
New Windsor Company.
Upper Three Runs Company.

Brig. Gen. Francis Marion's Brigade consisted of—
Lieut. Col. McDonald's Regiment.
Col. Richardson's   "
Col. Irwin's   "
Col. Benbow's   ".
Col. Maybank's   "

In Gen. Marion's Brigade, Jacob Brawler, who lived in the
present Marion County, and his 23 sons served ; he and 22 of
his sons were killed or died in service, and the one son who
survived came out of the war a cripple, and imbecile from
exposure and hardships.

LIST OF OFFICERS.

OF THE MILITIA OF SOUTH CAROLINA WHO TOOK PART IN
THE WAR OF THE REVOLUTION 1775–1783.

The sources from whence these names are obtained are
set opposite to their respective names. Very often several
of these authorities mention the same officer, and in this
list where double authorities are cited, it is because the
rank of the officer or the term of service has been of a different grade or different period.

In the citation of the Journal of the Council of Safety as
authority, these citations should very frequently have been
Journal of the Provincial Congress. When the Congress
was in session, the officers were appointed by it ; when it was
not in session, the Council of Safety appointed ; and hence
the Journal of the Council is cited merely for uniformity of
citation.

This list is doubtless very imperfect, but so many names
as are here gathered are by this list preserved from oblivion.

In preparing this list, aid has been received from many
friends, and acknowledgments are now made for such aid.
Mrs. Lucy H. Pickens, Miss S. P. Brownfield, Col. T. W.
Woodward, Major Harry Hammond, Mr. W. Ederington,
have all contributed to the names in the list. Major E.
Willis, of Charleston, who has probably the largest and best
collection in this State of histories, pamphlets, &c., relating
to the history of South Carolina, most kindly placed any
and all of his collection at the disposal of the Society, and
himself extracted and furnished a large number of names.

Name	Rank	Service / Expedition	Command	Reference
Abney, Nathaniel	Captain.			Gibbes's Documentary History, 19 Nov., 1775.
Alexa der, James	"			Johnson's Traditions of Revolution, 1781.
Allen, Jeremiah	Lieutenant.	Expedition under Major Williamson.		Gregg's History of Old Cheraws, 1782.
Allison, Robert	Captain.			Gibbes's Documentary History, 1781.
Allston, John	"			Jour. Coun. Safety, 30 Dec., 1775 Moul. Rev. 1778.
Allston, William				Gibbes's Documentary History, 1781.
Ancrum, —	Major.	Col. Peter Horry's Reg't Dragoons.	Marion Brigade.	Moultrie's Revolution, 1778.
Anderson, John	Captain.	Wounded.	"	Gibbes's Documentary History, 19 Nov., 1775.
Anderson, Robert	"	Expedition under Major Williamson.		"
Anderson, —		"		
Andrews, John	Adjutant.		Marion Brigade.	Ramsay's Revolution, 1780.
Adams, —	Lieut. Colonel.			Gregg's History of Old Cheraws, 1780.
Alt, Jacob	Captain.			
Bacot, Peter	"		Col. George Hick's Regiment.	Johnson's Traditions of Revolution, 1781.
Baddeley, John	Lieutenant.	Light Infantry Company.	South Carolina State Troops.	Gregg's History of Old Cheraws, 1782.
Baker, —	Captain.		Marion Brigade.	Jour. of Coun. of Safety, 22 Dec., 1775, Moultrie's
Barnwell, John	Colonel.		Charles Town Militia.	Gibbes's Doc. His., 1780. [Rev., 1778.]
Barnwell, Robert	Brig. General.	Beaufort Company.		Garden's Anecdotes, 1781.
Barry, John	Captain.			Moultrie's Revolution, 1779.
Barton, —	"			Johnson's Traditions of Revolution, 1780.
Baxter, —	Major.	Wounded Quinby Bridge, 1782.	Col. William Harden's Command.	Gibbes's Documentary History, 1781.
Beal, —	Lieutenant.			Moultrie's Revolution, 1781.
Beaty, —	Captain.			Gibbes's Documentary History, 1781.
Bennett, —	"			Gibbes's Documentary History, 1781.
Benson, —	Lieutenant.			Lossing's Field Book of Revolution, 1780. [His., 1780.
Bentham, James	Colonel.	Wounded near Nelson's Ferry.	Marion Brigade.	Frost's Field Book of Rev., 1781. Gibbes's Dec.
Benton, Sam	Captain.		Charles Town Militia.	Journal of Council of Safety, 22 Dec., 1775.
Beresford, Matthew	"	Expedition under Major Williamson.	Marion Brigade.	Gibbes's Documentary History, 1781.
Beresford, —	"	Prisoner at St. Augustine.		Gibbes's Doc. His., 1781.
Birk, —				
Bleakney, John	Major.	St. David's Parish.	Aide to Gen. William Moultrie.	Johnson's Traditions of Revolution, 19 Nov., 1775.
Blenford, —	Captain.		Marion Brigade.	Gibbes's Documentary History, 1781.
Bocquet, —	"			Journal of Council of Safety, 20 November, 1775.
Bonneau, —	Lieutenant.		Marion Brigade.	Gibbes's Documentary History, 1781.
Bond, —	"			"
Boward, —	Captain.	Wounded Savannah, 9 October, 1779.		Ramsay's Revolution, 1779.
Bonnetheau, Peter	Lieutenant.	" Eutaw, 8 September, 1781.		1781.
Bowman, —	"			Gibbes's Anecdotes, 1780.
Boykin, Samuel	Captain.	Battalion of Artillery.	Charles Town Militia.	Garden's Anecdotes, 1781.
Brandon, T	Col. mel.			Ramsay's Revolution, 1780.
Bratton, William		Company of Catawba Indians.		Journal of Council of Safety, 14 Jan., 1776.
Britton, Daniel	Lieutenant.	Dragoons.		Johnson's Tradition of Revolution, 1779.
Brown, Henry	"	Capt. Port's Co. Vols. St. David's Parish		Lossing's Field Book of Revolution, 1781.
Brown, Archibald	Captain.	Company of Volunteers.		Journal of Council of Safety, 20 Nov., 1775.
Brown, —	"	Light Infantry Company.	Charles Town Militia.	21 Feb., 1776.
				Johnson's Tradition of Revolution, 1776.
				Gibbes's Documentary History, 1781.
Brown, Tarleton	Lieutenant.	Wounded Stono, 1779.	Col. William Harden's Command.	Moultrie's Revolution, 1781.
	Captain.			Johnson's Traditions Revolution, 1781.

Name	Rank	Service / Event	Reference
Bruneau, —	Lieutenant.	Killed Savannah, 9 October, 1779.	Col. Isaac Hayne's Register, 1779.
Buckholdt, Abraham	Major.		Gregg's History of Old Cheraws, 1775.
Buckholdt, Peter	Captain.		Capt. Liming's Order Book, 1776.
Bull, Stephen	Colonel.		Journal of Council of Safety, 6 Dec. 1775.
Bull, —	Captain.		25 Jan., 1776.
Burton, Sam	Lieutenant.	Capt. Port's Co. Vols. St. David's Parish.	30 Nov., 1775.
Butler, James	Captain.		
Butler, John		Col. Benton's Reg't, Marion Brigade.	Johnson's Traditions of Revolution, 1776.
Butler, Pierce	Major.		Gregg's History of Old Cheraws, 1781.
Butler, William	Captain, Colonel.		Johnson's Traditions of Revolution, 1780.
Butler, William	Lieutenant.		Gilbee's Documentary History, 1781.
Butler, —	Major.		Johnson's Traditions of Revolution, 1780.
Barnett, Jacob	Lieutenant.	Col. Maham's Reg't Light Dragoons.	Moultrie's Revolution, 1778.
Bosquin, William		"	1782.
Bryan, John	Cornet.	"	"
Barnett, William	Adjutant.		"
Bachelor, Garner	Captain.		1781.
Benton, —	Lieutenant.		
Baxter, —	Captain.	Wounded Quinby Bridge. Cannon's Volunteers.	Journal of Council of Safety, 1 Dec., 1775.
Cannon, Daniel	Lieutenant.		" "
Cantey, —	Captain.		Johnson's Traditions of Revolution, 1783.
Caters, William	Lieutenant.	Volunteer Company, Beaufort. [Rovers.	Journal of Council of Safety, 26 Feb. 1776.
Cater, Thomas	Captain.		Gilbee's Documentary History, 1781.
Clark, —	Lieutenant.	Capt. John Allen's Foot Rangers, or Pon Pon Company.	Journal of Council of Safety, 11 Feb., 1776.
Cleze, —		Capt. John Allen's Foot Rangers, or [Rovers.	30 Jan., 1776.
Childred, Charles	Captain.		16 Dec., 1775.
Coachman, James			15 " "
Coachman, —		Ordnance Storekeeper. Expedition under Major Williamson.	" "
Cochran, Robert	Captain.		Gibbee's Documentary History, 19 Nov. 1775.
Colson, Jacob		Col. Benton's Reg't, Marion Brigade.	Gregg's History of Old Cheraws, 1781.
Conn, Thomas			Wallace's History of Williamsburg Church, 1780.
Conyers, Daniel	Adjutant.		Journal of Council of Safety, 11 Jan., 1776.
Conyers, James	Captain.	Round O Volunteers.	Gilbee's Documentary History, 1781.
Cook, Wilson (with- (drawn)	"		Johnson's Traditions of Revolution, 1780.
Cooper, S.	Lieutenant.		Gregg's History of Old Cheraws,
Corley, John	Major.		Journal of Council of Safety, 25 Dec., 1775.
Council, —	Lieutenant.	Capt. William Butler's Company.	Gibbee's Documentary History, 1781.
Couturier, John	Captain.		Lossing's Field Book of Revolution, 1780.
Cowan, —		Wounded Eutaw, 8 September, 1781.	Johnson's Traditions of Revolution, 1781.
Cranshead, —			Lossing's Field Book of Revolution, 1781.
Crawford, Robert	Major.	Killed Fort Motte, 1781.	Gilbee's Documentary History, 1781.
Crawford, —	Lieutenant.		Journal of Council of Safety, 18 Jan., 1776.
Cruzer, —	"	Wounded at Eutaw, 8 September, 1781 Capt Edward Howden's Company.	1782.
Culpeper, —	"	Col. Maham's Reg't Light Dragoons.	Gregg's History of Old Cheraws,
Cunningham, Arthur	"		Journal of Council of Safety, 21 Feb., 1776.
Campbell, Robert (mis)	"		1781.
Capers, William	Captain.		Gregg's History of Old Cheraws,
Dallas, Joseph	Ensign.	St. David's Parish.	Journal of Council of Safety, 21 Feb., 1776.
Daniel, — ron	Captain.		14 Jan., "

Name	Rank	Service / Company	Command	Authority
Danell, John	Captain.			Moultrie's Revolution, 1778.
David, John	Lieutenant.	Volunteer Company, St. David's Parish.	Marion Brigade.	Gregg's History of Old Cheraws, 1780.
Davis, Henry	"	"	Col. G. G. Powell's Regiment.	Journal of Council of Safety, 21 Feb., 1776.
Davis, Ransom	"	"	Col. G. G. Powell's Regiment.	" "
Davis, William	Captain.	Volunteer Company, St. David's Parish.	Marion Brigade.	Gibbes's Documentary History, 1781.
Deal, ——		Wounded Stono, 1779.	Col. G. G. Powell's Regiment.	Journal of Council of Safety, 21 Feb., 1776.
DeSaussure, Daniel	Lieutenant.	Volunteer Company, Beaufort.		Ramsay's Revolution, 1776.
Dewitt, Charles	Captain.			Harper's Memoir, 1776.
Dillard, James	Lieutenant.		Marion Brigade.	Gregg's History of Old Cheraws, 1781.
Doharty, James	Captain.	Killed near Beaufort.		Johnson's Traditions of Revolution, 1781.
Dozier, John	"	Volunteer Company, St. David's Parish.	Col. G. G. Powell's Regiment.	Moultrie's Revolution, 1776.
Dubose, ——	"		Marion Brigade.	Journal of Council of Safety, 21 Feb., 1776.
Dubose, Andrew	"		"	Moultrie's Revolution, 1758.
Dubose, Elias	"			Gregg's History of Old Cheraws, 1781.
Dupont, ——	Lieutenant.	German Fusileers.	Charles Town Militia.	Siegling's Centennial Oration, 1776.
Durham, Chamel	"			Ederington's Recollections, 1780.
Daxter, B.	Captain.			
Drayton, Thomas	Lieutenant.			Ederington's Recollections, 1780.
Ederington, Francis	Cadet.		Marion Brigade.	Gregg's History of Old Cheraws, 1781.
Ellerbee, Thomas	Quartermaster.			Journal of Council of Safety, 28 Dec., 1775.
Elliott, Benjamin	Captain.		Colleton County Regiment.	" 17 "
Elliott, Thomas	"			
Ellison, Samuel	Lieutenant Colonel.			Moultrie's Revolution, 1778.
Ellison, ——	Major.	Wounded Eutaw, 8 September, 1781.	South Carolina State Troops.	Gibbes's Documentary History, 1781.
Ervine, John	Lieutenant.			Wallace's Hist. of Wmbg Ch. Gibbes's Doc. His.
Erwin, James	Colonel.		Col. Kothmaler's Regiment.	Journal of Council of Safety, 18 Jan., 1776.
Eubank, John	Lieutenant.	Volunteer Company, St. David's Parish.	Col. G. G. Powell's Regiment.	" 29 Nov., 1775.
Evans, Charles	Ensign.		Col. Ilick's Reg't, Marion Brigade.	" 21 Feb., 1776.
Evans, Enoch	Captain.	Capt. Irby's Company.		Gregg's History of Old Cheraws, 1781.
Evans, George	Lieutenant.	"		1781.
Elliott, Thomas	A. D. C., Gen. Marion.			
Edwards, John	Judge Advocate.			Garden's Anecdotes.
Elliott, John	Captain.	Killed Ransom's Mills.		Journal of Council of Safety, 11 Jan., 1776.
Eally, ——		Commissary General and Paymaster.		Johnson's Tradition of Revolution, 1780.
Farr, Thomas, Jr.	Captain.			Journal of Council of Safety, 1 Dec., 1776.
Farrow, Thomas	Lieutenant.	Charles Town Rangers.	Craven County Regiment.	Journal of Council of Safety, 16 Dec., 1775.
Fenwicke, Thomas		Capt. Archibald McDaniel's Company.	Colleton County Regiment.	Capt. Lining's Order Book, 1776.
Fitzgerald, John	Major.			Lessesne's Field Book of Revolution, 1780.
Ford, George	Lieutenant.	St. David's Parish.	Col. G. G. Powell's Regiment.	Journal of Council of Safety, 21 Feb., 1776.
Fletcher, ——		Capt. Benjamin Marion's Company.	Berkeley County Regiment.	Capt. Lining's Order Book, 1776.
Ford, James	Captain.	Capt. Wigfall's Company.		Journal of Council of Safety, 1 Dec., 1775.
Fazattie, James	Captain.	Capt. Lining's Company.		Garden's Anecdotes.
Fazattie, Joseph	Lieutenant.	Indian Field Company.		Journal of Council of Safety, 1 Dec., 1775.
Freer, Charles	Captain.	Capt. Powell's Company.	Berkeley County Regiment.	
Fuller, Nathaniel	Lieutenant.	Wounded Quinby Bridge, 1781.		" 18 Jan., 1776.
Fullerton, John	Captain.	St. David's Parish.		
Futhy, William	Lieutenant.			Journal of Council of Safety, 21 Feb., 1776.
Fox, ——	"			
Gallaway, James				

Name	Rank	Company	Regiment / Brigade	Reference
Gamble, John	Major.		Marion Brigade.	Wallace's History of Williamsburg Church, 1780.
Garden, John	Lieutenant.	Williamsburg County.	Berkeley County Regiment.	Journal of Council of Safety, 1 Dec., 1775.
Garden, —	Colonel.	Capt. Wigfall's Company.		Moultrie's Revolution, 1775.
Gay, —	Lieutenant.		Marion Brigade.	Gregg's History of Old Cheraws, 1781.
Gee, —	Captain.			Ramsay's Revolution, 1781.
Gibbes, William Hasell	Capt., Lieutenant.	Wounded Eutaw, 8 Sept., 1781.	Charles Town Militia.	Garden's Anecdotes, 1776.
Giles, —	Captain.	Battalion Artillery.	South Carolina State Troops.	Gibbes's Documentary History, 1781.
Gillespie, —		Wounded Eutaw, 8 Sept., 1781.		Gregg's History of Old Cheraws.
Gillon, Alexander	Captain.	German Fusileers.	Charles Town Militia.	Sieghling's Centennial Oration, 1776.
Glover, Joseph	Colonel.		Colleton County Regiment.	Journal of Council of Safety, 9 Dec., 1776.
Gordunan, Joseph	Quartermaster.			Revolutionary General Assembly.
Godbolt, James	Lieutenant.	Capt. Peter Buckholt's Company.	Craven County Regiment.	Capt. Lining's Order Book, 1776.
Gordon, Roger	"		Marion Brigade.	Wallace's History of Williamsburg Church. 1781.
Gough, John	"	Capt. James Skirving's Company.	Berkeley County Regiment.	Capt. Lining's Order Book, 1776.
Gough, Richard	Captain.			Garden's Anecdotes.
Gough, —	"	Volunteer Company, St. David's Parish.	Marion Brigade.	Gibbes's Documentary History, 1781.
Grass, Joseph	Lieutenant.	Britton's Neck.	Col. G. G. Powell's Regiment.	Journal of Council of Safety, 21 Feb., 1776.
Green, —	Captain.		Col. Ervin's Regiment.	Gregg's History of Old Cheraws, 1780.
Gunn, Joseph	"	Capt. Postell's Company.	Charles Town Militia.	Jour. of Coun. of Safety, 26 Feb., 1776. Moultrie's
Griml...d, Thomas	Major.			[Rev., 1781.
Gerham, —	Captain.			
Geist, —	Lieutenant.			
Geezy, —	Colonel.			
Gilvert, —	Major.			
Green, J.	Captain.	Expedition under Major Williamson	Artillery.	Garden's Anecdotes.
Hall, George Abbott	"			Jour. Coun. Safety, 23 Dec., '75. Gibbes's Doc. His.
Hamilton, Andrew	"			Gibbes's Documentary History, 18 Nov., 1775.
Hamilton, Joseph	"			Johnson's Traditions of the Revolution.
Hammond, George	"			Jour. of Coun. of Safety, 21 Jan., 1776.
Hammond, John	Lieutenant.	Wounded Eutaw, 8 September, 1781.	State Troops, South Carolina.	Lossing's Field Book of Rev., 1750. Gibbes's Doc.
Hammond, LeRoy	Captain.		"	Gibbes's Documentary History, 1781. [His. 1781.
Haumond, Samuel	"	Expedition under Major Williamson.		Johnson's Traditions of Revolution.
Hammond, —	"	Artillery Company, Beaufort.		Jour. of Coun. of Safety, 26 Feb., '76, Gibbes's Doc.
Hampton, Edward	Ensign.	Col. William Harden's Regiment.		Gibbes's Doc. His., 1781. [His., 1781.
Hampton, Henry	Captain.	St. David's Parish.		Journal of Council of Safety, 21 Feb., 1776.
Harden, William	Colonel.			
Harden, —	Captain.			
Hardyman, Joseph	Lieutenant.	St. David's Parish.		Moultrie's Revolution, 1775.
Hardyman, Thomas	Colonel.	Pee Dee.		Journal of Council of Safety, 9 Jan., 1781.
Harlest n, John	Lieutenant.			" 21 Feb. "
Hargrave, Robert	Major.	Col. Richard Hampton's Regiment.		Gregg's History of Old Cheraws, 1780.
Hargrave, Samuel	Captain.			Moultrie's Revolution, 1775.
Harlow, Benjamin	Colonel.			O'Neall's Annals of Newberry.
Harrington, Wm. Henry	Colonel.			Gibbes's Documentary History, 1781.
Harris, —	Lieutenant.			Mills's Statistics, South Carolina.
Harris, Abijah	Major.			Lossing's Field Book of Revolution, 1780.
Hart, Merrill	Captain.			Moultrie's Revolution, 1781.
Harvey, Thomas	Colonel.			
Hawthorne, —	"			
Hayes, —				

Name	Rank	Company / Command	Regiment / Brigade	Source
Hayne, Isaac	Colonel.	Pon Pon Company.	Marion Brigade.	Jour. of Coun. of Safety, 15 Jan., '76, Gibbes's Doc. Gregg's His. Old Cheraws, 1782. [His., 1781.
Hendricks, William	Lieutenant.	Capt. Peter Buckholt's Company.	Craven County Regiment.	Capt. Lining's Order Book, 1776.
Heron, —	Captain.	Volunteer Company, Beaufort.		Journal of Council of Safety, 29 Feb., 1776.
Heyward, Daniel, Jr.	Ensign.	" "		
Heyward, John	Captain.	Battalion of Artillery.	Charles Town Militia.	Moultrie's Revolution, 1776. [Old Cheraws, 1781.
Heyward, Thomas, Jr.	Major.			Jour. Coun. of Safety, 18 Feb., '76. Gregg's His.
Hick, George	Colonel.			Lossing's Field Book of Revolution, 1780.
Hill, William	Lieutenant.			Gregg's History of Old Cheraw, 1780.
Hinds, —				
Hird, John	Major.	Round O Company.	Marion Brigade.	Moultrie's Revolution, 1778.
Hogg, —	Lieutenant.			
Holding, Matthew	"	Capt. Robert Lide's Company.	Col. G. G. Powell's Regiment.	Journal of Council of Safety, 21 Feb., 1776.
Hollis, Moses	"	Killed Eutaw, 8 September, 1781.	Col. Benson's Regiment.	Gregg's History of Old Cheraws, 1782.
Holmes, —	Colonel.	Charles Town Volunteers.	Marion Brigade.	Ramsay's Revolut n, 1781.
Horry, Hugh	Captain.			Lossing's Field Book of Revolution, 1781.
Hoger, John				Gibbes's Documentary History, 1776.
Huggins, John	Lieut. and Adjutant.	Artillery Company, Beaufort.	Col. Hugh Giles's Regiment.	Gregg's History of Old Cheraws, 1779.
Huggins, Benjamin	Lieutenant.		Col. Peter Horry's Reg't Dragoons.	Gibbes's Documentary History, 1781.
Hughes, Thomas	Colonel.	Expedition under Major Williamson.		Journal of Council of Safety, 27 Nov., 1775.
Hughes, —	Captain.			Johnson's Traditions of Revolution, 1780.
Hunter, David	"			Gibbes's Documentary History, 13 Nov., 1775.
Hyrne, Henry	Lieutenant.	Killed Musgrove Mills.	Col. George Hick's Regiment.	Journal of Council of Safety, 25 Dec., 1775.
Hoss, —	Captain.			Johnson's Traditions of Revolution, 1780.
Inman, S.	"		Marion Brigade.	Gregg's History of Old Cheraws, 1780.
Irby, Edmund	Colonel.		Col. Geo. Hick's Reg't, Marion Brig.	Lossing's Field Book of Revolution, 1780.
Irvin, —	"		Col. Kolb's.	Moultrie's Revolution, 1781.
Irwin, —			" "	Gregg's History of Old Cheraws, 1782.
Jackson, John (Lake.	Lieutenant.		" "	[1780.
Jackson, Stephen	Captain.			Wallace's History of Williamsburg Church, 1770,
James, Alexander	Lieutenant.			
James, John (Lake.	Captain.			Gibbes's Documentary History, 1779.
James, John, Jr., of the	Major.	Edisto Island Volunteer Company.	Colleton County Regiment.	Captain Lining's Order Book, 1776.
Jamieson, —	Captain.	St. Helena Island Volunteers.		Journal of Council of Safety, 11 Feb, 1776.
Jenerct, Jacob	Ensign.	Edisto Island Volunteers.	Col. Rothmaler's Regiment.	" " 7 Dec., 1776.
Jenkins, Benjamin	Captain.		Colleton County Regiment.	" 9 Jan., 1776.
Jenkins, John	Lieutenant.		Col. Kolb's Reg't, Marion Brigade.	" 11 Feb., 1776.
Jen-ins, Joseph			Col. Rothmaler's Regiment.	
Jenkins, Joseph	Captain.		Col. Benton's Reg't, Marion Brigade.	Gregg's History of Old Cheraw, 1782.
Jenkins, Reuben	Lieutenant.	Col. William Harden's Command.		Journal of Council of Safety, 9 Jan., 1776.
Jenkins, Thomas	Captain.		Col.G.G. Powell's Reg't, Marion Brig.	Gregg's History of Old Cheraw, 1782.
Jinkins, James	Ensign.			Johnson's Tra. Rev. '80. [Book Rev. 1781.
Johnson, Richard	Captain.	Artillery Company, Beaufort.		Jour. Coun. Safety, 21 Feb., 1776. Lossing's Field
Johnson, William	Major.	Expedition under Major Williamson.		Johnson's Traditions of Revolution, 1780.
Joiner, John	Captain.		Marion Brigade.	Gibbes's Documentary History, 19 Nov., 1775.
Jolley, —	Lieutenant.	Wagon Master General.	Col. Rothmaler's Regiment.	Gregg's History of Old Cheraws, 1781.
Jones, Adam C.	Captain.	Capt. Benjamin Marion's Company.	Col. Singleton's Regiment.	Journal of Council of Safety, 9 Jan., 1776.
Jones, Edward	Ensign.			2 Dec., 1776.
Jordan, Jonathan				25 Dec., 1776.
Kolloch, Michael				
Karn, Thomas				

Name	Rank	Company / Service	Regiment / Brigade	Authority
Kee, Thomas	Captain.	Capt. Daniel Linder's Company.	Berkeley County Regiment,	Johnson's Traditions of Revolution, 1781.
Kelly, Daniel	Lieutenant.			Captain Lining's Order Book 1776.
Kelly, James				O'Neall's Annals of Newberry.
Kershaw, Joseph	Colonel.			Moultrie's Revolution, 1776.
Kimbrough, John	Captain.	Com'y of Volunteers, St. David's Parish.	Col. G. G. Powell's Regiment.	Journal of Council of Safety, 30 Nov. 1775.
Kincaid, James	"	Cavalry.		Mill's Statistics South Carolina.
King, George	"		Col. G. G. Powell's Regiment.	Journal of Council of Safety, 21 Feb. 1776.
Kirkburn, ...				Gibbes's Documentary History, 1891.
Knight, James, Sr.	Lieutenant.	Com'y of Volunteers, St. David's Parish.	Col. G. G. Powell's Regiment.	Journal of Council of Safety, 30 Nov. 1775.
Koger, Jno. (withdrawn)	Captain.	Round O Volunteers	Colleton County Regiment.	Journal of Council of Safety, 11 Jan. 1776.
Kolb, Abel	Colonel.			Jour. Coun. Safety 21 Feb. 1776. Gibbes' Doc.
Kunnill, Joseph	Lieut. Colonel.	Killed Savannah, 9 October, 1779.	German Fusileers, Charles Town Mil.	Sterling's Cent. Oration, 1724. [His. 1781.
Kendoll, Frederick	Colonel.		Col. Postell's Regiment.	1781.
Lacy, Edward	Lieutenant.	King's Mountain.		Lossing's Field Book of Revolution, 1780.
Ladson, Abraham	Captain.	Capt. Benjamin Marion's Company.	Colleton County Regiment.	Captain Lining's Order Book, 1776.
Ladson, Thomas	Major.	John's Island Company.	Marion Brigade.	Journal of Council of Safety, 2 December, 1775.
Ladson, ...	Captain.			Gibbes's Documentary History, 1781.
Land, ...		Expedition under Major Williamson.		Garden's Anecdotes.
Langdon, Thomas	Lieutenant.	Prisoner St. Augustine.	Charles Town Militia.	Gibbes's Documentary History, 19 November, 1775.
Lee, William	Captain.	Light Infantry Company.		Johnson's Tradition of Revolution, 1780.
... Benjamin	"			Journal of Council of Safety, 31 Jan, 1776.
... Samuel	"		Marion Brigade.	Gibbes's Documentary History, 1781.
Lenud, —	"		"	
Liddle, Moses	Major.	St. David's Parish.	Col. G. G. Powell's Regiment.	Johnson's Traditions of Revolution, 1781.
Little, Thomas	"		Craven County Reg't, Marion Brig.	Journal of Council of Safety, 21 Feb, 1776.
Lide, Robert	"		Berkeley County Regiment.	Gregg's His. Old
Lander, Daniel	"			Capt. Lining's Order Book, 1776. [Cheraws, 1775.
Lining, ...				Journal of Council of Safety, 1 December, 1775.
Lindsey, John	Colonel.			O'Neall's Annals of Newberry.
Lisle, ...				Moultrie's Revolution, 1775.
Lothrop, R.	Lieutenant.	German Fusileers,	Charles Town Militia.	Mid'. Statistics South Carolina.
Livingston, William	Captain.	Capt. James Skirving's Company,	Berkeley County Regiment,	Seigling's Centennial Oration, 1780.
Lloyd, Martin	Lieutenant.	Expedition under Major Williamson.		Captain Lining's Order Book, 1776.
Logan, Francis	Captain.			Gibbes's Documentary History, 19 November, 1775.
Logan, George	"			Mill's Statistics South Carolina.
Love, ...				Johnson's Traditions of Revolution, 1780. [Rev. 1781.
Lush, ...				Gibbes's Doc. His., 1781. Johnson's Tra.
Lushington, Richard	Adjutant.	Killed Eutaw, 8 September, 1781.	South Carolina State Troops.	Jour. Coun. Safety 22 Dec, 1775.
Lykes, Arcanaus	Lieut.		Charles Town Militia.	Edrington's Recollections.
Lykes, James	Colonel.			O'Neall's Annals of Newberry.
Lykes, John	"			
Lyon, Gatbridge	Captain.		Col. Benton's Reg't, Marion Brigade	Gregg's History of Old Cheraws, 1781.
Lyon, William	Lieutenant.		Sumter Brigade.	Gibbes's Documentary History, 1781.
Lewis, W.	"			
Macady, John	Captain.	Wounded Eutaw, 8 September, 1781,	Berkeley County Regiment.	Wallace's History of Williamsburg Church, 1780.
Marion, Benjamin	"	Artillery, killed siege of Augusta.	South Carolina State Troops.	Jour. Coun. of Safety, 22 Dec., 1775. Capt. Lining's
Martin, John	Major.			Gibbes's Doc. His. '81. [Order Book, 21 April, '76.
Martin, William	"			Lossing's Field Book of Revolution, 1781.

Name	Rank	Company / Unit	Regiment	Reference
Matthews, Benjamin	Lieutenant.	John's Island Company.	[Colleton County Regiment.]	Journal of Council of Safety, 2 December, 1775.
Matthews, John Raven	"			Johnson's Traditions of Revolution, 1779.
Maxwell,—	Major.,			Garden's Anecdotes.
Maybank, Joseph	"		Berkeley County Regiment.	Journal of Council of Safety, 30 January, 1776.
Mazyck, Stephen	Lieutenant.			1 December, 1775,
Megge, or Magee, Elisha	"	Captain Ravenel's Company.	Col. G. G. Powell's Regiment.	21 February, 1776,
Middleton, Thomas, Jr	"	St. David's Parish.	Berkeley County Regiment.	1 December, 1775.
Middleton,—	Lieut. Colonel.	Captain Smith's Company,	South Carolina State Troops.	
Mitcell, Juan	Lieutenant.	Wounded Eutaw, 1 September, 1781.	Marion Brigade.	Gibbes's Documentary History, 1781.
Miller, John D	"		Berkeley County Regiment.	Gregg's History of Old Cheraws, 1781.
Miller, Stephen	Lieut., Colonel,	Battalion of Artillery.	Marion Brigade.	Garden's Anecdotes, 1781.
Mitchell,—	Captain,			Journal of Council of Safety, 31 January, 1776,
Moffit, —	"			Gibbes's Documentary History, 1780,
Morgan, William	Lieutenant.	Battalion of Artillery.	Charles Town Militia.	Lossing's Field Book of Revolution, 1780.
Moody, Charles	"	St. David's Parish.	Col. G. G. Powell's Regim't.	Garden's Anecdotes.
Moore,—	Captain.		South Carolina State Troops.	Journal of Council of Safety, 21 February, 1776.
Mnaw, Henry	"	Kingstree Company.		Gibbes's Documentary History, 1781.
Munnerlyn, James	Lieutenant.		Marion Brigade.	Wallace's History of Williamsburg Church, 1780.
Murphy, Maurice	Captain,		Col. G. G. Powell's Reg't, Marion	Journal of Council of Safety, 21 Feb., 1776, [Brig.
Murrell,—	Lieut. Colonel.		Col. Hick's Reg't,	Journal of Council of Safety, 21 Feb., 1776.
May, Benjamin	Captain.	Christ Church Company.		Gibbes's Documentary History, 1781.
Moultrie, Alexander	Lieutenant.		Charles Town Militia.	
Mann, John	Captain.	Musketeers.	Col. Richardson's Regiment.	Journal of Council of Safety, January 22, 1776. 1776.
Melton,—	Lieutenant.	Killed Strawberry.		1781.
Maurac,—	Major, Colonel.			
Muller, Albert A	Captain.	Expedition under Major Williamson. [Horse.	Marion Brigade.	Gibbes's Documentary History, 19 November, 1775.
McCall, James	Lieutenant.	Ramsey says "Col McCall of the Lt.	South Carolina State Troops.	Gregg's History of Old Cheraws, 1781.
McCall, Hugh	Captain.	Killed Hanging Rock,—, 1780.		Carrington's Est. Rev. So. Johnson's Tra. Rev. '80.
McCall, Hugh	Ensign.			Lossing's Field Book of Revolution, 1780.
McClure, John	Captain.	Expedition under Major Williamson.		
McClure,—	"		Marion Brigade.	Wallace's History of Williamsburg Church, 1780.
McCottrey, William	"			Gibbes's Documentary History, 15 November, 1775.
McCreery, Robert	Lieut. Colonel.		Marion Brigade.	Gregg's History of Old Cheraws, 1782.
McCullouch, George	Major.			Captain Lining's Order Book, 1776.
McDaniel, Archibald	Captain.		Col. Benton's Reg't, Marion Brigade	Carrington's Battle of Revolution, 1780.
McDonald,—	"			Gregg's History of old Cheraws, 1781.
McDowell,—	"			Johnson's Traditions of Revolution, 1780.
McIntosh, Alexander	Lieut. Colonel.	Col. William Hardin's Command.		Gibbes's Documentary History, 1781.
McJunkin, Joseph	Major.			Lee's Memoirs, 1781.
McKay,—	Captain.	Company of Volunt'rs, St David's Parish	Marion Brigade.	Johnson's Traditions of Revolution, 1780.
McLachlin,—	"		Charles Town Militia.	Journal of Council of Safety, 20 November, 1775.
McTier,—	Lieut., Colonel.		Col. G. G. Powell's Regiment.	Gregg's History of old Cheraws, 1782.
McManus, Thomas	Captain.	The Rangers.		Journal of Council of Safety, 1 December, 1775,
McMuldrough,—	Lieutenant.	St. David's Parish.		21 February, 1776.
McQueen, John	Captain.			
McRae, Duncan	Lieutenant.			P.M.
McK..d	Captain.			
Macleeleod, William	Captain.	St. David's Parish.	Col. G. G. Powell's Regiment.	Journal of Council of Safety, 21 Feb., 1776.
Neavill, Isaac	Lieutenant.			

Name	Rank	Service / Company	Unit	References
Neil, Thomas	Colonel.	Killed Rocky Mount, ——, 1780.	Charles Town Militia.	Journal of Council of Safety, 7 Nov., 1775, 1780. Wallace's History of Williamsburg Church. Garden's Anecdotes.
Nelson, John	Captain.	Battalion of Artillery.		Moultrie's Revolution, 1776.
Neuville, Edward	Lieutenant.	Stono Company.	Colleton County Regiment.	Journal of Council of Safety, 23 Jan., 1776. Johnson's Traditions of Revolution, 1780.
Newman, —	Captain.	Expedition under Major Williamson, Prisoner at St. Augustine.		Gibbes's Documentary History, 19 Nov., 1775. Johnson's Traditions of Revolution, 1780.
Nichols, Henry	Ensign.		Marion Brigade.	Gregg's History of Old Cheraws, 1782. Gibbes's Documentary History, 1781. 1775.
Nixon, John	Lieut. Colonel.			
Noble, Alexander	Captain.			
North, Edward				
Norwood, John	Captain.	Round O Company, Capt. Daniel Lauder's Company.	Colleton County Regiment. Berkeley County Regiment.	Journal of Council of Safety, 17 Jan., 1776. Captain Lining's Order Book, 1776.
Odingsell, —				
O'Neill,				
Oswald, William	Lieutenant.	Wounded Savannah, 9 October, 1779. Of Horse.	Marion Brigade.	Mill's Statistic. South Carolina. Ramsey's Revolution, 1779. Gregg's History of Old Cheraws, 1782. 1781.
Ott, Abraham				
Ott sen. Samuel	Captain.			
Parker, —	Lieutenant.			
Parrott, Thomas	Captain.			
Pasley, Robert				
Pearson, John	Major.	Wounded Eutaw, 8 September, 1781. St. David's Parish.	Col. Benton's Reg't Marion Brigade	Mills, Statistic, South Carolina. Gregg's History of Old Cheraws, 1781. Ramsey's Revolution, 1781.
Pearson, Moses	Captain.	Killed Siege of Ninety-Six, ——, 1781.	Col. G. G. Powell's Regiment.	Journal of Council of Safety, 21 Feb., 1776. Lossing's Field Book of Revolution, 1780. National Portrait Gallery, 1781.
Pegues or Pegues, Claudius	Ensign.			
Perkins, David	Brig. General.			
Pickens, Andrew	Captain.			
Pickens, Joseph				
Pinckney, John	Lieutenant.	Militia Rangers, Volunteers, Killed Eutaw, 8 September, 1781.	Col. Hicks's Reg't, Marion Brigade, Col. Rothmaler's Regiment, 10th Regiment, new acquisition.	Gibbes's Documentary History, 1781. Gregg's History of Old Cheraws, 1781. Journal of Council of Safety, 18 Jan., 1776. [1781. Jour. Coun. Safety, 1 Nov. 75. Gibbes's Doc. Hist. Lossing's Field Book Rev., 1781. Moultrie's Rev.
Pledger, John	Captain. Colonel.			
Plowder, Edward				
Polk, Ezekiel	Lieutenant.		Marion Brigade.	
Polk, William	Major, Colonel.			
Postell, James	Captain.			
Postell, John	Colonel.			
Powell, Gabriel G	Lieutenant.	Wounded Stono, ——, 1779. Light Infantry Company. Volunteer Company, St. David's Parish	Marion Brigade.	Journal of Council of Safety, 16 Feb., 1776. Ramsey's Revolution, 1779. Journal of Council of Safety, 21 Feb., 1776. Gregg's History of Old Cheraws, 1780. 1781.
Prince, —	Captain.			
Prioleau, Heat	Lieut. Colonel.			
Prior Lake	Lieutenant.			
Purvis, John	Captain.			
Parker, John	Lieut. Colonel.			
Price,				
Post, John	Captain.	Killed Quinby Bridge. Wando Company. Prisoner at St. Augustine.	Berkeley County Regiment.	Journal of Council of Safety, 10 December, 1775. Johnson's Tradition of Revolution, 1780. Captain Lining's Order Book, 1776.
Perry,	Captain.			
Queleh, Andrew	Captain.			
Raven,l,				
Read, Jacob		Expedition under Major Williamson. Volunteer Company, St. David's Parish. Captain Post's Company.		Gibbes's Documentary History, 19 November, 1775. Journal of Council of Safety, 30 November, 1775.
Redmond, John				
Keel, George	Lieutenant.			
Keen-lds, John				
Reynolds, Richard				
Rhodes,				[1780.
Richardson, Richard	Colonel. General.			Garden's Anecdotes. Jour. Coun. Safety, 2 Dec. 75. Johnson's Tra. Rev. 26 December, 1775.
Richardson, Richard, Jr	Captain. Colonel.		Marion Brigade.	Gibbes's Documentary History, 1781.
Richardson William				

Name	Rank	Company / Service	Brigade / Regiment	Reference
Richardson, —	Lieut. Colonel.		Charles Town Militia.	Gibbes's Documentary History, 1781.
Robinson, George	Captain.			Journal of Council of Safety, 25 February, 1776.
Roche, Patrick	Ensign.			22 December, 1775.
Rodgers, John	Captain.			Gibbes's Documentary History, 19 November, 1775.
Rothmaler, Job	Colonel.	Expedition under Major Williamson.		Johnson's Traditions of Revolution, 1780.
Rowe, Henry	"			Journal of Council of Safety, 2 December, 1775.
Rushing, John	Captain.	St. Mark's Parish.		Captain Lining's Order Book, 1776.
Rutherford, —	Lieutenant.			Gregg's History of Old Cheraw, 1782.
Rutledge, Edward	Major.	Discharged 12 April, 1781.		Gibbes's Documentary History, 1781.
Rutledge, Thomas	Captain.	Col. Benton's Reg't, Marion Brigade		Johnson's Traditions of Revolution, 1776.
Ryan, James	Adjutant.	South Carolina State Troops.		Journal of Council of Safety, 13 February, 1776.
Ryan, Albert	Lieutenant.	Charles Town Militia.		Johnson's Traditions of Revolution, 1780.
Rogers, —	Ensign.	Granville County Regiment.		1781.
St John, Andrew	Captain.		Colonel Richardson's Regiment.	
Sanders, William	Lieutenant.	Pon Pon Company.		Journal of Council of Safety, 16 December, 1775.
Saunders, Nathaniel	Colonel.	Round O Company.	Colleton County Regiment.	Jour. Coun. Safety, 27 Jan., 1776. Gibbes's Doc.
Savage, John	Lieutenant.		Col. Benton's Reg't, Marion Brigade	Gregg's His. Old Cheraw, 1781. Gibbes, 1781.
Sawyer, —	"			Journal of Council of Safety, 7 December, 1775.
Scott, Joseph	"			Monltrie's Revolution, 1778.
Scriven, —	Colonel.	The Rangers.	Charles Town Militia,	Wallace's History of William-burg Church.
Sharp, James	Lieutenant.	Killed Savannah, 9 October, 1779.	German Fusil's, Charles Town Mil'a	Gibbes's Documentary History, 1781.
Shepherd, —	Captain.	Light Infantry Company.	Charles Town Militia.	Journal of Council of Safety, 1 Dec, 1775.
Shubrick, Thomas, Jr	Ensign.	Killed Eutaw, 8 September, 1781.		Monltrie's Revolution, 1779.
Simons, —	Lieutenant.			Journal of Council of Safety, 31 Jan, 1776.
Simons, Keating	Brig. Major.		Marion Brigade.	Ramsay's Revolution, 1781.
Simons, Maurice	Colonel.			Garden's Anecdotes, 1781.
Simpkins, Arthur	Captain.			Monltrie's Revolution, 1778.
Sinclair, —	"			Mill's Statistics South Carolina.
Singleton, John	"		Marion Brigade.	Monltrie's Revolution, 1778.
Singleton, Matthew	"			Johnson's Traditions of Revolution 1780.
Singleton, —	Colonel.			Journal of Council of Safety, 28 Dec, 1775.
Sumterfield, Francis	Captain.	Expedition under Major Williamson.	Berkeley County Regiment.	1 Dec, 1775.
Skirving, James	Colonel.		Berkeley County Regiment.	Gibbes's Documentary History, 19 Nov, 1775.
Skirving, —	Captain.	Expedition under Major Williamson.		Captain Lining's Order Book, 1776.
Sham, John	"			Monltrie's Revolution, 1778.
Smith, Aaron	Lieutenant.	Volunteer Company, St. David's Parish.	Berkeley County Regiment.	O'Neill's Annals of Newberry.
Smith, Benjamin	"	St. George Company.	Col. G. G. Powell's Regiment.	Gibbes's Documentary History, 19 Nov, 1775.
Smith, Samuel	"			Journal of Council of Safety, 21 Dec, 1775.
Smith, Thomas	"			21 Feb, 1776.
Snizer, —	Captain.		Marion Brigade.	1 Dec, 1775.
Snipe, William Clay	"	Wounded Eutaw, 8 September, 1781.	Marion Brigade. Sumter Brigade.	Gibbes's Documentary His, 1781.
Snow, William	Lieutenant.			Jour. Coun. Safety, 27 Jan, 1776. Gibbes's Doc.
Spozens, —	Captain.	St. David's Parish.	Col. Benton's Reg't, Marion Brigade	Gibbes's Documentary History, 1781.
Sparks, Daniel	Lieutenant.	Wounded Parker's Ferry, 31 Aug, 1781.	Colonel G. G. Powell's Regiment.	Gregg's History of Old Cheraw, 1781.
Spivey, George	Colonel.	Volunteer Company, St. David's Parish.	Col Benton's Reg't, Marion Brigade	Journal of Council of Safety, 21 Feb, 1781.
Statford, —	Ensign.			Jour. Coun. Safety, 20 Nov, 75.
Standard, William	Captain.		Marion Brigade.	Johnson's Traditions of Revolution.
Starke, John	Lieutenant.			Gibbes's Documentary His, 1781.
Stephens, —				

Name	Rank	Company / Regiment	Reference
Stevens, Daniel	Lieutenant.	Battalion of Artillery.	Johnson's Traditions of Revolution.
Stevens, Jervis Henry	Captain.		Garden's Anecdotes.
Stone, Benjamin	"	Charles Town Militia. Col. H. Maham's Regiment.	Journal of Council of Safety, 21 December, 1775
Steward, Chas. Augustus	Lieut. Colonel.		Gregg's History of Old Cheraws, 1775.
Strobel, Daniel	Lieutenant.	Charles Town Militia.	Siegling's Cent Oration, 1779
Strother, George	"	German Fusileers.	Gregg's History of Old Cheraws, 1781
Sutton, John	Ensign.	Marion Brigade.	Journal of Council of Safety, 21 Feb, 1776
Sutton, Robert	Captain.	Capt Robt Lide's Co. St. David's Parish Colonel G. G. Powell's Regiment.	9 Jan, 1776
Swinton, —	Major.		
Simons, James	Captain.	Wounded Quinby bridge, —, 1782.	Moultrie's Revolution, 1781
Smith, James	Lieutenant.	Col Maham's Reg't Light Dragoons.	1782.
Sayler, —			
Sinkler, —			
Screven, T.			
Taylor, James	Colonel.		Johnson's Traditions of Revolution, 1775
Taylor, Thomas	Captain.		Lossing's Field Book Rev., '80. Moultrie's Rev., '81
Telfout, Tunis	Colonel.	Artillery Company, Beaufort.	Journal of Council of Safety, 21 Nov, 1775
Templeman, —	Lieutenant.		Mill's Statistics South Carolina.
Terrell, James	Captain.		Gregg's History of Old Cheraws, 1782.
Terrell, Samuel	Lieutenant.		
Thomas, Edward	Colonel.	Col. Benton's Reg't, Marion Brigade	Gregg's History of Old Cheraws, 1782. 1781.
Thomas, John	"	Colonel Singleton's Regiment.	Journal of Council of Safety, 22 Dec, 1775.
Thomas, John, Jr.	Captain.		Johnson's Tra. Rev., '80. 7 Nov, 1775.
Thomas, Robert	Major.		Johnson's Traditions of Revolution, 1780.
Thomas, Tresham	Major.	Capt Benj. Marion's Company.	Gregg's History of Old Cheraws, 1781.
Thompson, Jas., (with- drawn)	Major.	Col Benton's Reg't, Marion Brigade Colleton County Regiment.	Journal of Council of Safety, 11 Jan, 1776
Thornby, —	Captain.		Gregg's History of Old Cheraws, 1780
Timmon, John	Lieutenant.		Mill's Statistic South Carolina.
Toomer, Anthony	Captain.	Round O Company.	Johnson's Traditions of Revolution, 1775
Toomer, Joshua			Moultrie's Revolution, 1781
Trapier, Paul		Charles Town Militia.	Journal of Council of Safety, 26 Feb, 1776.
Turner, —			Moultrie's Revolution, 1781
Turner, Sterling		Battalion of Artillery,	Johnson's Traditions of Revolution, 1780.
Thetus, James		Artillery Company, Georgetown.	1782
Taylor, Samuel	Lieutenant.		
Tunnicase, Henry	Lieutenant.	Col Maham's Regiment Light Dragoons	
Thetus, Perrin	Surgeon.	"	
Thompson, Thomas	Major.		
Thompson, J.	Lieutenant.	Colonel Richardson's Regiment.	1776
Thompson, —	Colonel.		1777
Tate, —	Lieutenant.		1781
Tenhimen, James	Captain.		1781
Vanderhorst, Arnoldus	Lieutenant.		1781
Vulcan, Peter	Lieutenant.	Captain — Ravenel's Company. Wounded Savannah, 9 October, 1779 John's Island Company. Prisoner at St. Augustine.	
Wale, —			
Wahit, Abraham	Ensign.	Berkeley County Regiment. Wounded Savannah, 9 October, 1779 St. David's Parish.	Journal of Council of Safety, 25 Dec, 1775
Wakefield, John		Colleton County Regiment.	Ramsay's Revolution, 1779
Wilkcie, —	Lieutenant.		Journal of Council of Safety, 1 Dec, 1775
Wall, Wright	Lieutenant.	Col G. G. Powell's Regiment. Charles Town Militia.	Johnson's Traditions of Revolution, 1780.
Warham, Charles	Adjutant.	Battalion Art'y, killed Charles Town '80.	Ramsay's Revolution, 1779 Journal of Council of Safety, 21 Feb, 1776. Ramsay's Revolution, 1790.

	Marion Brigade.	Gibbes's Documentary History, 1781, Journal of Council of Safety, 1 Dec., 1775.
St. George's Company		
	South Carolina State Troops.	O'Neall's Annals of Newberry. Johnson's Traditions of Revolution, 1780. Garden's Anecdotes, 1776.
Battalion of Artillery. Artillery.	Charles Town Militia Marion Brigade.	Gibbes's Documentary History, 1781. Johnson's Tradition of Revolution, 1780. Garden's Anecdotes, 1776.
Battalion of Artillery St. David's Parish.	Charles Town Militia. Col. G. Powell's Regiment Col. Benton's Reg't, Marion Brigade.	Journal of Council of Safety, 21 Feb. 1776. Gregg's History of Old Cheraws, 1781. Garden's Anecdotes, 1779.
Wounded Savannah, 9 October, 1779. Battalion Art'y, killed Port Royal, 1778.	Col. Benton's Reg't, Marion Brigade. Charles Town Militia.	Gregg's History of Old Cheraws, 1782, Gibbes's Documentary History, 1771 Ramsay's Revolution, 1785. Moultrie's Revolution, 1778. Gibbes's Documentary History, 1781. 19 Nov., 1775.
Expedition under Major Williamson.	Col. Benton's Reg't Marion Brigade.	Gregg's History of Old Cheraws, 1782 Carrington's Battles of the Revolution, 1780. Journal of Council of Safety, 30 Nov, 1775.
Killed King's Mountain, —— 1780. Snow Campaign 1775, Commander.	Col. Benton's Reg't, Marion Brigade. Col. G. G. Powell's Regiment.	Gregg's History of Old Cheraws, 1782 Journal of Council of Safety, 21 Feb., 1776.
St. David's Parish.	Col. Koff's Reg't, Marion Brigade;	Gregg's History of Old Cheraws, 1782. Lossing's Field Book of the Revolution, 1780. Jour Coun. Safety, 21 Feb., '76. Gibbes's Doc. His. Wallace's His. Williamsburg Church, 1781. [1781. Journal of Council of Safety, 30 Nov., 1775. 16 Jan., 1776. 2 Dec., 1775.
Indian Co. of Foot Rangers or Rovers.	Marion Brigade-	
Capt. Thos. Port's Co., St. David's Par.		Gibbes's Documentary History, 19 Nov., 1775.
John's Island Company; Expedition under Major Williamson.		Johnson's Traditions of Revolution, 1780. Mills Statistics South Carolina.